Hattie
and the Fox

by Mem Fox
Illustrated by Patricia Mullins

Hattie was a big black hen.
One morning she looked up and said,
"Goodness gracious me!
I can see a nose in the bushes!"

"Good grief!" said the goose.
"Well, well!" said the pig.

"Who cares?" said the sheep.
"So what?" said the horse.
"What next?" said the cow.

And Hattie said,
"Goodness gracious me!
I can see a nose
and two eyes in the bushes!"

"Good grief!" said the goose.
"Well, well!" said the pig.
"Who cares?" said the sheep.
"So what?" said the horse.
"What next?" said the cow.

And Hattie said,
"Goodness gracious me!
I can see a nose, two eyes,
and two ears in the bushes!"

"Good grief!" said the goose.
"Well, well!" said the pig.
"Who cares?" said the sheep.
"So what?" said the horse.
"What next?" said the cow.

And Hattie said,
"Goodness gracious me!
I can see a nose, two eyes, two ears,
and two legs in the bushes!"

"Good grief!" said the goose.
"Well, well!" said the pig.
"Who cares?" said the sheep.
"So what?" said the horse.
"What next?" said the cow.

And Hattie said,
"Goodness gracious me!
I can see a nose, two eyes, two ears, two legs,
and a body in the bushes!"

"Good grief!" said the goose.
"Well, well!" said the pig.
"Who cares?" said the sheep.
"So what?" said the horse.
"What next?" said the cow.

And Hattie said,
"Goodness gracious me!
I can see a nose, two eyes, two ears, a body, four legs,
and a tail in the bushes!
It's a fox! It's a fox!"
And she flew very quickly into a nearby tree.

"Oh, no!" said the goose.
"Dear me!" said the pig.
"Oh, dear!" said the sheep.
"Oh, help!" said the horse.

But the cow said, "MOO!"

so loudly that the fox was frightened and ran away.

And they were all so surprised
that none of them said anything
for a very long time.

Aladdin Paperbacks
An imprint of Simon & Schuster
Children's Publishing Division
1230 Avenue of the Americas
New York, NY 10020
First Aladdin Paperbacks edition, 1992
Also available in a hardcover edition from
Simon & Schuster Books for Young Readers
Printed in China
0316 SCP
40 39

Library of Congress Cataloging-in-Publication Data
Fox, Mem, 1946-
     Hattie and the fox / by Mem Fox ; illustrations by Patricia
Mullins. — 1st Aladdin Books ed.   p.   cm.
     Summary: Hattie, a big black hen, discovers a fox in the bushes,
which creates varying reactions in the other barnyard animals.
     ISBN 978-0-689-71611-9
     [1. Chickens—Fiction. 2. Foxes—Fiction. 3. Domestic animals—
Fiction.] I. Mullins, Patricia, 1952-   ill.
[PZ7.F8373Hat   1992]   91-41727
[E]—dc20